D1505935

DISCARDED

• Eleanor Koldofsky •

Clip-Clop

illustrated by David Parkins

Tundra Books

Text copyright © 2005 by Eleanor Koldofsky
Illustrations copyright © 2005 by David Parkins

Published in Canada by Tundra Books,
481 University Avenue, Toronto, Ontario M5G 2E9

Published in the United States by Tundra Books of Northern New York,
P.O. Box 1030, Plattsburgh, New York 12901

Library of Congress Control Number: 2004115971

Library and Archives Canada Cataloguing in Publication

Koldofsky, Eleanor, date
Clip-clop / Eleanor Koldofsky ; illustrated by David Parkins.

ISBN 0-88776-681-1

1. Draft horses – Juvenile fiction. I. Title.

PS8571.O686C55 2005   jC813'.54   C2004-906644-7

ONTARIO ARTS COUNCIL
CONSEIL DES ARTS DE L'ONTARIO

We acknowledge the financial support of the Government of Canada through the
Book Publishing Industry Development Program (BPIDP) and that of the Government
of Ontario through the Ontario Media Development Corporation's Ontario
Book Initiative. We further acknowledge the support of the Canada Council for
the Arts and the Ontario Arts Council for our publishing program.

The illustrations for this book were rendered in watercolor and ink on paper.

Design: Kong Tik Njo

Printed in Hong Kong, China

1 2 3 4 5 6   10 09 08 07 06 05

Author's Note

At the turn of the 20th century, horses were willing workers, good company, and common sights on city streets. They pulled delivery wagons, carted away junk, and brought a smile to many faces with their familiar presence. They would eventually give way to faster, more comfortable means of transportation, but nothing would ever replace the sounds and beauty of the gentle *clip-clop* horses.

Today we call people who work hard and steadily *workhorses*, and the fond memory of those faithful servants lives in many hearts. To one little girl, the animals were simply friends who marked her day and gave her the feeling that she was never alone. This book is a tribute to the wide array of beasts who may have differed in size, color, and conformation, but who shared the work of humans for as little as a bag of oats and perhaps a warm blanket at the end of the day.

To my grandchildren, Zachary, Jhase, Cosmo, and Echo – and to theirs.   – E.K.

To Jane, Adam, Rachel, and Jessica.   – D.P.

Criminentlies! The *clink* of bottles and the *clip-clop* of iron horseshoes on pavement sent Consuela scurrying outside. It was her job to trade empty milk bottles for full, and she couldn't be late. She got there just in time to say, "Good morning," and pat the horse on his velvet nose. He snuffled softly in her ear before the flap of reins told him to get a move on. *Clip-clop-clink, clip-clop-clink. See-you-tomorrow, clip-clop-clink.*

As the sun rose higher, Consuela heard another sound. The *quick-trot, clippety-clop,* of the beautiful brown horse could mean only one thing. The tea wagon was coming, and today it was in a hurry. Consuela was never wrong. The red, gold, and black painted wagon sped past on rubber tires. Consuela could hear the jingle of harness bells and the horse's heavy breathing as it hurried away. "Goodbye," she shouted after it.

"Straaaawberries — four boxes for a quarter! Banaaaanas — ten cents a basket! Potaaaatoes —

fifty cents a bag!" called the produce man. His wagon was drawn by a dappled gray mare. *Lolop . . . lolop . . . lolop.* Three neighbor ladies took their time picking over the fruit and vegetables, and agreeing to divide a hundred-pound bag of potatoes between them. The produce man saw Consuela pick up some carrots that had fallen and said she could keep them. Then, *lolop . . . lolop . . . lolop . . .* into the distance they went.

It was almost noon when down the road, Consuela saw a swaybacked black horse with wooden traces coming right up to his blinkers. He was bony and he dragged his feet –
s l ~ i ~ i ~ p ~ s l ~ o ~ o ~ p,
s l ~ i ~ i ~ p ~ s l ~ o ~ o ~ p.
The bearded old man behind him shouted, "Ra-a-a-gs! Bone-z-z-z! Bottles." They both looked hungry.

Clang-clang, rattle-clatter! Bells rang and a horn blared as a red fire wagon sped toward them, drowning out the call of the ragman. Everyone hurried out of the path of two huge Percherons that galloped as fast as they could.
Thumpety-thumpety-thump!
Out-of-the-way! Out-of-the-way!
Thumpety-thumpety-thump!
Their eyes rolled and their nostrils flared as they strained to get to the fire.

The wagon turned the corner on its wide wheels and was gone. When the dust cleared, Consuela noticed the tired black horse limping back into the center of the street. The ragman got down and picked up the horse's hoof. It had thrown a shoe in its scramble to get out of the way.

Consuela was first to spot the iron horseshoe lying in the road. She darted forward, snatched it up, and returned it to the man. A blacksmith could nail it back in place and the horse would be comfortable again. Consuela stroked him, but the thin horse was more interested in her bundle of carrots than anything else.

Without stopping to think, Consuela gave one and another and then another to the hungry animal. The ragman was touched by her kindness. He searched through his wagon until he found something special — a small, plaid baby blanket, *almost* new!

Consuela was thrilled. She ran into the house to show her mother. It was time to get money for the iceman, anyway. Out she came with a dime, still clutching her precious blanket.

The iceman didn't arrive until the sun was beginning to lose some of its heat. His Clydesdale was strong and shiny and moved at a good *clip-clipclop* as splashes of water dripped off the back in a straight, wet line. The driver had covered his huge blocks of ice with sackcloth to slow the melting. Consuela had her money ready. The man broke off an extra large piece with his ice pick in exchange for her dime.

With rusty tongs he carried it into the house and put it in the icebox. When he returned, the children who were sneaking ice chips from the wagon scurried away. The iceman winked and offered a chip to Consuela, his only paying customer, before lifting the heavy iron "anchor" from the sidewalk. With a toss of his head, the big Clydesdale continued on his way. *Clip-clipclop, clip-clipclop.*

Consuela's fingers tingled with cold as she licked the ice. The feeling reminded her that the coal and kindling wagons would soon start making their rounds. The calls of, "W-o-o-o-d!" and, "C-o-o-a-a-l!" and the heavy **CLAP-clop-clop** of the big dray horses would mingle in the crisp air and echo off building walls.

Small sackcloth bags would hold the kindling, a hundred pounds of coal would cost twenty-five cents. The big horses never minded their heavy loads or the warm clouds that puffed from their nostrils and jeweled their eyelashes. Consuela missed them, even if she didn't miss her own frost-nipped toes.

Unfamiliar footsteps jerked Consuela back to the present. The dainty *clippety-clippety-clippety* was coming nearer. This was a horse Consuela had never heard before. She wheeled around. Her eyes settled on a beautiful little pony. A pinto pony! Walking beside it was a camera man carrying a tripod from which a sign dangled.

Oh, if she could only sit on the pony. Just one sit. But where in the world would Consuela ever get twenty-five cents? She tried not to think about it as the kids and mothers came out, one by one.

Tony took pictures of all the children wearing his sombrero encircled with pom-poms. When he was finished, he looked around to make sure there were no other customers. He noticed Consuela with her big brown eyes, and wanted to photograph her.

He smiled, his glance shifting to the blanket still clutched in her hand. Consuela's eyes flashed a little spark of hope. She instantly held the blanket out. Tony accepted the bargain, plopped the hat on her head, and swept her onto the pony's back.

Consuela sat ramrod straight astride the pony with her red sandals in the stirrups and a grin from ear to ear. The plaid blanket peeked out from the saddlebag as Tony snapped the photo. "Picture perfect!" he declared, bowing low to Consuela.

Consuela nodded regally. She had never been happier. She would keep her picture forever to remember this wonderful *clip-clop* day. The day she was a cowgirl . . . who felt just like a princess!